HIPPOGRIFF FEATHERS

by

Bob Stanish

illustrated by Bob Stanish

Copyright © Good Apple, Inc. 1981

ISBN No. 0-86653-009-6

GOOD APPLE, INC.
BOX 299
CARTHAGE, IL 62321

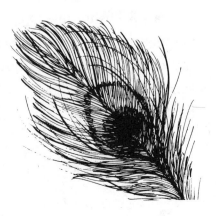

DEDICATION

This book is dedicated to my daughter Lindley,
who awoke us in time to escape a burning house
and to son Jon, whose fervent belief in
the value of all creatures, great and small,
storybook and real, gave me the inspiration
for this.

ACKNOWLEDGEMENTS

Special Thanks To:

Bob Eberle and **Jean Peek**
for their Foreword;
Earl Stone for his poem,

and to:

Cynthia Anderson	Carolyn Hartley
Marilyn Baker	Katherine Herr
Barbara Boston	Shirley Hudson
Karen Brewer	Ralph Moore
Hazel Broughton	Virginia Nottingham
Pat Connelly	Marjorie Robertson
Pat Courtwright	Pat Sawyer
Pat Craig	Sara Schlichting
Julia Fetter	Victoria White

for the field testing of the book materials,

and to:

Ruth Noller
Dorothy Sisk
Alison Strickland
and
Andy Yancey
for their reviews.

FOREWORD

Introducing the work of a colleague of many years' standing is a unique experience. In many ways it is like saying, "I want you to meet a friend of mine." To know Bob Stanish is to know his convictions. His beliefs are reflected in his work. For sure, he does not view thinking as a spectator sport. He feels that it is a shame for talent to be wasted. Every person should have the opportunity to develop his potential to the fullest. Through his work, he is saying that complex ways of thinking must be taught and learned. Thinking processes are not mastered by reading definitions in a reference book. In his previous work, **SUNFLOWERING, I BELIEVE IN UNICORNS,** and **THE UNCONVENTIONAL INVENTION BOOK,** the author built a bridge of thinking processes which linked understanding to application. In this work the span is strengthened with a systematic design for assisting children to improve their creative thinking and problem-solving skills.

In taking complex thinking processes and shaping them for use with children, the author has demonstrated his mastery of the metaphor, synectics, description, and checklisting. His questioning stimulates one's imagination and prompts an immediate response, for example: What things are made more beautiful by age? (I wish it were me.) What things are green and cannot be eaten? (Maybe a greenhouse.) What goes pit-a-pat? (Rain on the roof, of course.) What can get squishy? (That wasp that I swatted in the office.)

It is important to note that correct or best answers are not stressed by the author. Rather, the emphasis is placed on the production of imaginative ideas. With ample space provided for responding, again and again students are encouraged to stretch their imaginations in search for ideas.

The intent of the author has been to provide ways for cultivating and enhancing the thinking processes. However, the author has also provided ways for cultivating and enhancing the feeling processes. This is done with reference to self-concept, good feelings, personal qualities, and being-the-thing analogies. This amounts to applying cognitive processes to affective concerns. The author cares for those that create. His particular concern is for the development of potential creators and problem solvers. Through his writing he shares the wisdom he has gained through his own teaching, writing, and creating. He has acknowledged that the fulfillment and actualization of the individual comes about when one is able to harmonize one's own creation with creation in other forms. This book stands in testimony of his belief that there is no path to progress apart from solving problems and the acceptance of creativity as a means of finding better ways.

Bob Eberle, author and consultant
2 Brookside Court
Edwardsville, Illinois 62025

Authentic aesthetic experiences, creative actions, are part of our daily lives: These are no mystery, no obtuse theory, no convoluted model but are actual. Intent does not make art. Only practical invention is basic, competent, and artistic. We may admire inventions of the past but our lives pale when we insist art, creativity, is the stuff of museums. It is not, never was, may not be. We may build theories, models, and curricula based on what we wish life was like, some past or future blue sky; but that which we experiment with, dirty our hands with daily, that is our art. Once in a while we get a chance to touch another's dreams and processes and we are taught. This happens in this book. Bob Stanish and his **HIPPOGRIFF FEATHERS** teaches us a way to go which will be our way as we grow and expand beyond the gentle experiences Bob suggests. Teaching and learning is art, is basic.

Most educational experiences claim sequence but have no part of that intuitive continuity that makes learning real and artistic. We in curriculum planning must try to share our skills and change as much as we plan change. The greatest part of being a teacher is the letting go of the learner so that the learner plays, experiments, with our suggestions until learner becomes teacher. Both are then artistic, creative, and alive. Neither are dull. Democracy is enslaved by the "basic competencies" which clone lemmings from unicorns; a safe democracy (a *discordia concors* in poetry and synectics symbolic analogy?) must go down a steep spiral to tribal totalitarianism. When we remove our art from our hands and tongues, when we place art in museums for the sake of worship, then we destroy lovely democratic ambiguities and invention. Museums are for the short run.

Actually, schools and curriculums are for the short run. Human beings seem to have the potential for lasting. Lasting is possible only when we see creative thinking and problem solving as basic, dirty, and beautiful. More formal structures are binary: yes and no; right and wrong; inferior and superior; A and F. Informal, lasting learning involves clusters of related activities fermenting without limit. John Dewey (in Art as Experience) said: "In order to understand the meaning of artistic products, we have to forget them for a time, to turn aside from them and have recourse to the ordinary forces and conditions of experience that we do not usually regard as aesthetic." We must cultivate more than one mode of thought to guide our approach to active, creative imagining. Though society rewards a substantive and internally consistent mode identified as logical, rational, and factual and suspects the intuitive, inventive mode of the metaphor and song, we must join effect and cognition, right and left hemispheres, female and male. Schooling must not be cloning but art come to by a divine human articulation of plan and dream. **HIPPOGRIFF FEATHERS** combines organization with expansion. In it, Bob Stanish demands no ends, only adventures. From it, the learner creates daily life anew as art: personal, flawed, expanding, and inventing.

Jean W. Peek, Ph.D.
Language Arts Coordinator
Williamsville Central School
Williamsville, New York, 14221

ODE TO A HIPPOGRIFF

A Hippogriff loves to explore and play.

He makes the most of every day.

He flies up high,

Wanders away,

Gazes at the sky,

Wants me to stay.

I wish I were a Hippogriff-

'Cause I also love to explore and play.

 Earl Stone

ABOUT USING THIS BOOK...

HIPPOGRIFF FEATHERS is divided into seven chapters. Each chapter deals with a particular methodology for developing creativity and sharpening problem-solving skills.

Each chapter, as a lead-in to the student activities, outlines the following sections:

GETTING ORIENTED - a background on the methodology to give you some idea as to purpose and usage.

GETTING STARTED - helpful hints and suggestions on how to use and what to expect from the activities.

WHAT ELSE - ways to follow up or extend the activity concept, in other words, where else to take it!

ONE MORE THING ABOUT THIS BOOK . . . The introductory page to each chapter and many of the student activity pages have a larger than normal letter size. Use these pages for making overhead projector transparencies for in-service training sessions with your fellow teachers or for parent groups. Help spread the word that creative thinking and the skills of problem solving are among the most basic human skills.

MAKING BEST USE OF THIS BOOK

What follows are some suggestions for making the best use of the book activities. These suggestions will also increase your skills as a developer of student creative thinking and problem-solving skills.

SUGGESTION ONE: DEFER JUDGMENT AND INCUBATE!

Make **DEFERRING JUDGMENT** (Parnes and Harding, 1962); (Osborn, 1963) a teaching and learning principle.

1.   During brainstorming or when student ideation is in effect, **DEFER JUDGMENT.**

2.   After student ideation, allow **TIME FOR INCUBATION.** New associations and modifications of ideas will result.

3.   Screen ideas by having students **DEVELOP AND USE CRITERIA.**

SUGGESTION TWO: USE BRAINSTORMING!

BRAINSTORMING (Osborn, 1963) is a group method of generating a quantity of ideas in a short period of time. Follow these suggestions:

1.   **ACCEPT EVERYTHING!** Withhold criticism or evaluation of the ideas - in other words, defer judgment.

2.   **WELCOME THE OUTLANDISH!** New ideas are born only when the freedom to hatch them exists. Encourage the wild and different!

3.   **ENCOURAGE QUANTITY!** Good ideas only come from a lot of ideas.

4.   **PARTICIPATE WITH THE KIDS!** When students are brainstorming, you contribute too! Your addition to the pool of ideas will add excitement to the process.

5.   **BUILD AND COMBINE!** Combine two or more ideas into a third idea.

SUGGESTION **THREE**: WATCH YOUR QUESTIONING!

Teacher questions can frighten or excite, intimidate or stimulate, expand or restrict. It depends a lot on how they are asked!

1. **ASK OPEN-ENDED QUESTIONS.** Questions of this type have no one "right" response but call for a multitude of responses. Try questions like: "What if . . . all plant life was colored red?" " . . . there was no salt in the oceans?" " . . . decay was not a process?" Use these kinds of beginnings: "How many ways can you think of to . . . ?" "What would you do if . . . ?" "What might happen if . . .?" "In what other ways . . .?"

2. **ASK FEELING QUESTIONS.** Encourage students to examine their emotions and values with questions like: "How do you feel about . . . ?" "Can you explain the way you feel about . . . ?" "What 'ing' words would best describe the way you feel?" "What makes this important to you?"

3. **ASK QUESTIONS OF A METAPHORICAL NATURE.** Look at ideas or things from different angles by asking questions like: "In what ways is a mountain like a memory?" "In what ways might I feel and act if I were a polluted molecule of water?" "Which is quicker, a noun or a pronoun?"

SUGGESTION **FOUR**: INVENTORY CREATIVE THINKING!

As students venture into activities such as those in this book, stop occasionally and inventory their creative thinking skills (Torrance, 1962).

1. **FLUENT THINKING** is generating a quantity of responses.

2. **FLEXIBLE THINKING** is generating different categories of thought.

3. **ELABORATE THINKING** is adding embellishment or detail to an idea.

4. **ORIGINAL THINKING** is coming up with solutions that others do not normally think of.

REFERENCES

Osborn, Alex F., **Applied Imagination** (3rd. Ed.). New York: Scribner's, 1963

Parnes, Sidney J., and Harding, Harold F., (ed.), **A Source Book for Creative Thinking.** New York: Scribner's, 1962.

Torrance, E. Paul, **Guiding Creative Talent**. Englewood Cliffs, New Jersey: Prentice-Hall, 1962.

Hippogriffs only compete with their own potential!

THE IDEA RATING GUIDE

Use the GUIDE for

 DEVELOPING AN EVALUATIVE CRITERIA;

 SELECTING THE BEST IDEA FROM AMONG MANY IDEAS;

 STRENGTHENING ANALYSIS, SYNTHESIS, AND EVALUATIVE THINKING SKILLS.

EFFECT ON...?   AVAILABILITY?   performance?   TIME?

COST?   RISKS?   efficiency?   APPLICATION?

THE IDEA RATING GUIDE

GETTING ORIENTED:

A major concern has always been the lack of follow-through on classroom brainstorming sessions. The purpose of brainstorming is to produce many ideas or possible solutions to a problem within a short period of time. What is needed is a way to select the best ideas from the quantity of ideas produced.

Check out the **Creative Actionbook** by Ruth B. Noller, Sidney J. Parnes, and Angelo M. Biondi, (Noller, Parnes, and Biondi, 1976), for information on idea rating charts. For additional information on how to use them within classrooms see **It's a Gas To Be Gifted,** (Noller, Treffinger, and Houseman, 1979), and **CPS for Kids,** (Eberle and Stanish, 1980).

GETTING STARTED:

Refer to the sample IDEA RATING GUIDE in this chapter. Notice that the problem begins with the phrase, "in what ways ...?" Structuring questions in this manner is an effective way of providing for the quantitative production of ideas. Parallel to each idea are squares that contain a point value. The point values are arbitrarily determined by weighing each of the criterion factors against the ideas listed. The point values are then totaled to determine which idea(s) are best.

Distribute copies of the GUIDE and do a five-minute brainstorming session on the same problem cited in the sample with your class. Use a simple voting procedure like a show of hands for the best five or six choices and have students write them under the "ideas" section on their GUIDES. Do another brainstorming session in three minutes on ways or standards by which the ideas could be measured (criteria). Encourage your class to vote on the four best to represent the criteria. Individually or as a class determine point values for each idea as measured by the criteria. Total the points in the last column for idea selection.

Advise students to be sure to word the criterion statements either all positive or all negative. Otherwise conflicting point values will occur.

WHAT ELSE

As students become more proficient with the development and usage of criterion, encourage them to use more than four items. By drawing additional lines or by using two IDEA RATING GUIDE sheets, this can easily be accomplished.

Encourage students to use the IDEA RATING GUIDE with personal problems. Encourage students to form small groups and use the GUIDE on common or class problems. Encourage students to take copies of the GUIDE home and explain the procedures to their parents for problem solutions germane to families.

REFERENCES

Eberle, Bob, and Stanish, Bob. **CPS for Kids**. Buffalo, New York: D.O.K. Publishers, 1980.

Noller, Ruth B., Parens, Sidney J., and Biondi, Angelo M., **Creative Actionbook**. New York: Scribner's 1976.

Noller, Ruth B., Treffinger, Donald J., and Houseman, Elwood D. **It's a Gas to be Gifted or CPS for the Gifted and Talented**. Buffalo, New York: D.O.K. Publishers, 1979.

7

Idea Rating Guide

problem:

In what ways can I improve my ability to remember science facts in order to get passing grades on weekly tests?

ideas

ideas	Effect on other people's time?	Take away time from other things I have to do?	Hold my interest and attention?	Have enough time?	scoring column
Write science facts over and over again on paper.					
Have a family member help me.					
Study with friends.					
Write science facts on index cards and place in hip pocket. Look at them whenever I get the chance.					
Find some fun ways and games to help me remember.					
Get some family member to do my chores so I'll have more time to study science.					

scoring: 3 points — very workable!
2 points — somewhat workable!
1 point — not so workable!

Idea Rating Guide

criteria

problem:

scoring column

ideas

scoring: 3 points — very workable!
2 points — somewhat workable!
1 point — not so workable!

IDEA CHECKLIST

Use a **CHECKLIST** for

~ EXTENDING IDEA SUPPLIES.

~ PROVIDING SOLUTION POSSIBILITIES TO A PROBLEM.

~ SUGGESTING IMPROVEMENTS IN THINGS OR A PROCESS.

<u>Put to other uses</u>?...How many different uses? If modified?

<u>Adapt</u>?...What else is like this? What does it suggest?

<u>Modify</u>?...Change the meaning? Form? Texture? Shape? Motion? Color? Substance? Taste?

<u>Magnify</u>?...Make larger? Stronger? Longer? Thicker?

<u>Minify</u>? ...Make smaller? Lower? Shorter? Lighter?

<u>Substitute</u>? ...What else might work?

<u>Rearrange</u>? .. Can parts be shuffled for a different arrangement or sequence?

<u>Reverse</u>? ...Turn it backwards? Upside down? Inside out?

<u>Combine</u>? ...Place it with something else?

IDEA CHECKLIST

GETTING ORIENTED:

The CHECKLIST is versatile in its application. Although its major use is to suggest improvement in things, the statements may generate alternative and effective solutions to a wide variety of problems. The CHECKLIST strategy should be used to SUPPLEMENT and NOT REPLACE intuitive or natural ideation. Because of its value to expanding alternatives, it is suggested that the activities in this chapter be introduced to students early and not later in the book. It is also recommended that the activities be followed in sequence at periodic intervals over a week or two.

There are a number of CHECKLISTS in literature on creative thinking. This chapter contains an adaption of Alex Osborn's, "Idea-Spurring Questions," (Osborn, 1963). Two other highly regarded approaches are Bob Eberle's **Scamper,** (Eberle, 1971), which is a mnemonic arrangement of Osborn's list and Gary Davis' approach in **Psychology of Problem Solving,** (Davis, 1973).

GETTING STARTED:

It is recommended that the activities in this chapter are introduced as individual effort activities. Allow plenty of time after completion for total class sharing of ideas; then discuss or brainstorm other idea possibilities.

Put To Other Uses - A Table: After individual student completion on this two-page activity, brainstorm with the total class other possibilities.

Adapt: Use the same approach as above on this activity. Since the first two activities in this chapter deal with the concept of ideation, ideation should occur somewhat more naturally for the activities that follow.

Modify: First brainstorm or discuss with your class the shapes of various well-known product containers; then distribute the activity. Encourage students to share their drawings.

Magnify: Before beginning this activity, hold up a paper clip and ask: "If this could be made larger, what other functions might it serve?" Accommodate several responses; then distribute the activty. Provide sharing time afterwards.

Minify: Have students think of objects that could easily fill up a closet-size room, for example, a vacuum cleaner, a refrigerator, etc. Have them speculate as to what functions these objects might serve if they were reduced small enough to fit into a shoe box, for example, a small vacuum cleaner for removing lint from jackets; a small refrigerator that would operate off of an automobile battery, etc. Have students work this activity individually with full sharing time afterwards.

Substitute: Begin this activity by having students choose five items they could survive with in the wilderness. Question them as to what other functions these five items would have. A discussion of this type should provide the concept of substitution rather effectively. Distribute the activity and share results.

Rearrange: Discuss with your students the need at times to rearrange. Begin with the idea of classroom arrangements from small group work to individual work to class dramatic sketches to other kinds of activities. Indicate that at times there is a need to rearrange our lives, our habits, and our ways of doing things in order to solve problems. This activity deals with the latter. Provide plenty of time and follow-up with individual kinds of conferences as needed.

Reversing: Reversing things at times might be just the answer to a tough problem. This activity deals with this and also the usage of the right brain hemisphere. Reinforce the notion of not thinking too deeply about drawing a unicorn to look like a unicorn. Encourage students to just concentrate on the upside down lines and how they come together. Their drawing should also be upside down on their activity paper. Encourage students to draw two drawings. Practice makes thngs a little better. Afterwards ask if, in their opinions, the reversal aspect improved what they might have done right-side up? Encourage students to check it out.

For an excellent source on right brain hemisphere capabilities in art, locate **Drawing on the Right Side of the Brain**, (Edwards, 1979).

Combining: This activity should produce some inventiveness of thought. Tell students not to worry about how good their drawings are because the idea is the important thing. Look for flexibility of thinking in the items they added to the machine.

WHAT ELSE

Pose a question like, "In what ways can we reduce school vandalism?" Do a five-minute brainstorming session on the question. Be sure to record group responses. Afterwards, reintroduce the CHECKLIST items by asking: "What ideas from our list could we PUT TO OTHER USES? ADAPT? MODIFY? MAGNIFY? MINIFY? SUBSTITUTE? REARRANGE? REVERSE? COMBINE?" Observe how the initial ideas were extended and improved by using the CHECKLIST.

REFERENCES

Davis, Gary A. **Psychology of Problem Solving.** New York: Basic Books, 1972.

Eberle, Bob. **Scamper: Games for Imagination Development.** Buffalo, New York: D.O.K. Publishers, 1971.

Edwards, Betty. **Drawing on the Right Side of the Brain.** Los Angeles, California: J.P. Tarcher, Inc., 1979.

Osborn, Alex F. **Applied Imagination.** (3rd Ed.) New York: Scribner's, 1963.

Hippogriffs have developed a deep affection for all living creatures - great and small. This did not come easy. But then, things of great value seldom do!

13

Hippogriffs have always been able to distinguish the important things from the irrelevant. Viewing sunsets is a very important hippogriff activity.

Put To Other Uses — a table

new ways to use it as is —

snow sledding
_____
_____
_____
_____
_____
_____
_____

before breakfast exercises
_____
_____
_____
_____
_____
_____
_____

This activity continues on the next page.

Put To Other Uses —

new ways to use it if modified —

Turn it upside down and tie some chains to the legs. Hang from a tree limb and have a "table-swing."

_____
_____
_____
_____
_____
_____
_____
_____
_____
_____
_____
_____
_____
_____
_____

Adapt

what else is like this?

an ice pack

a balloon without air

_____

_____

_____

_____

_____

what other things does it suggest?

a coin purse without coins

_____

_____

_____

_____

_____

_____

_____

_____

Modify

change the meaning, the form, or the shape of a liquid container

Magnify

make larger: *function?*

a running shoe

_____ into _____ a small speed boat

_____ into _____

_____ into _____

_____ into _____

_____ into _____

_____ into _____

_____ into _____

_____ into _____

_____ into _____

What can be made larger by
making it smaller?

making motion picture film...

anything else?

19

make smaller:

_____a garden rake_____ into _____a back scratcher_____

_____ into _____

_____ into _____

_____ into _____

_____

_____

_____

_____

_____

_____

_____

What can be made smaller by
making it larger?

Blowing up
a balloon
until it bursts.

anything else?

20

Substitute

what ?

water skis

what else instead ?

a front door

The idea I'd most like to see my teacher

try is _____

_____

_____

_____

_____

Rearrange

arrangements that don't seem to fit:

Too much to do and not enough time.

rearrangements that might fit:

Homework after school; play time after dinner; TV after play time; review homework before bedtime and chores before school.

Use the back of this paper for more of the same.

Reversing

Take a look at this upside-down picture. Draw this picture upside down just as you see it.

While drawing the picture just concentrate on the lines and how they come together. Block the "upside-down" idea from your mind as you draw it.

Make sure your drawing is upside down.

Now rate your picture. Turn it "upside-right" and look at it. Is it a better picture than you would have normally drawn?

Combining

Combine a soda machine with a trash machine. How might they function together as a single machine?

Draw a picture or a diagram of the new machine and label the parts.

Now think of some other things to add to your new machine. Do it!

List things made more beautiful by age.

List things that cannot be seen.

LISTING

Use LISTING for

* EXPANDING ASSOCIATIONS;

* MAKING ANALOGIES;

* ACTIVATING VERBAL FLUENCY;

* HAVING FUN WITH IDEAS.

My list of ways to give a book report.
List things that are Mmmmm......!
List examples of a connecting – bond.

LISTING

GETTING ORIENTED: The LISTING technique is that of listing ideas associated in some way with a very general subject. Either as a total group, small group or as an individual student activity, LISTING will promote the stream of free associations to flow. LISTING is a fun way of starting or ending a school day. Encourage students to develop games with it. It is ideal for long car trips with parents and in those moments in which we are waiting in lines or contending with idle time. It is a way of activating intellectual processes that can be extremely beneficial later on in those moments when decision making and problem solving are required.

For added LISTING enjoyment see Margaret Holland and Alison Strickland's book, **The Listing Book**, (Holland and Strickland, 1978). For LISTING activities dealing with imagery see **Sunflowering**, (Stanish, 1977), and for valuing see **I Believe in Unicorns**, (Stanish, 1979). LISTING strategies with forced associations can be found in Angelo M. Biondi's (ed.) book, **Have an Affair With Your Mind**, in the chapter written by Charles S. Whiting, (Biondi, 1974).

GETTING STARTED: Be sure to introduce some of the LISTING activities before usage of the ATTRIBUTE LISTING techniques in the next chapter. LISTING promotes the necessary skills of expanding word and idea associations and making analogies that are so necessary to ATTRIBUTE LISTING.

Consider the following in selecting LISTING activities from this chapter: **List Things That are Green And Cannot Be Eaten:** This is a good one to begin with for a total group assault. The concept of piggy-backing on ideas generated by others will occur here. EMPHASIZE before and even during the brainstorming that all IDEAS ARE ACCEPTABLE! Don't allow criticism of any kind of student ideas.

List Ways You Could Feed Walnuts To A Hungry Monster Without Getting Too Close: This is an exercise for individual student use. Look for original ideas and encourage far-out thinking. Praise it when it occurs.

List Things That Can Really Stick: Another possibility for total or small group participation. Much the same instructions as in "List Things That Are Green ..."

List Things That Would Cause A Hippopotamus To Hyperventilate: Discuss what hyperventilation is and the symptoms accompanying it. Try it with either the total class, small groups or as an individual student activity. When the question arises, "What is a hippogriff?" - don't give any answers but do encourage curiosity.

List Things That Can Get Squishy: Another activity that can be used in any approach pattern you would like. Encourage the transfer of something tactile to things that are intellectually "squishy," like too many problems for one day, etc.

List Things That Go Pit-A-Pat: Try this as an individual student exercise for checking out individual fluency. Provide about 10 minutes or less to see which students are the most fluent by simply counting responses. Keep a log or a good memory and see if improvement occurs with a similar activity in a month or so. It should!

List Things That Could Become Nubbles: This one plays on the concept of things worn down by usage. Follow the activity with a question like, "What kinds of things might a civilization or a family wear down?" This activity is recommended for a small group effort.

List Things That You Feel Good About: This one gets into self-esteem. Use the results to learn more about your students. How we feel about things and ourselves determines how well we do almost anything. Some worth-knowing clues should result.

List Things That Might Become Squiggles: Same suggestions as were given for the "Nubbles" activity.

List Things _____: This one is for your students or you. Have fun with it!

WHAT ELSE Try LISTING techniques with academic concepts. For example, list words within words (elasticity = last, as, tic, city, it). List adjectives that begin with "s." List ways to slice a square in four equal parts. List ways you could prove the presence of ozone in the atmosphere.

After a LISTING activity, try having students categorize the responses into classification headings. Then ask, "What is the function of classification?"

REFERENCES

Biondi, Angelo M. (ed.) **Have an Affair With Your Mind**, Chapter 6, "Forced Relationship Techniques," by Charles S. Whiting. Great Neck, New York: Creative Synergetic Associates, Ltd., 1974.

Holland, Margaret and Strickland, Alison. **The Listing Book**. Columbus, Ohio: School Book Fairs, 1978.

Stanish, Bob. **Sunflowering: Thinking, Feeling, Doing Activities for Creative Expression**. Carthage, Illinois: Good Apple, Inc. 1977.

Stanish, Bob. **I Believe in Unicorns: Classroom Experiences for Activating Creative Thinking**. Carthage, Illinois: Good Apple, Inc. 1979.

Hippogriffs are sometimes mistaken for condors and even minotaurs. This is a very common mistake of the human species, that is, judging things from a distance.

LIST things
that are green and cannot be eaten.

_____

_____

_____

_____

_____ Green with envy can't be eaten. _____

_____

_____

_____

_____

_____

_____

_____

_____

_____

_____

_____

_____

____ poison ivy ____

_____

_____

_____

_____

_____

_____

_____

Inflated green balloons can't
be eaten!

LIST ways
you could feed walnuts to a hungry monster without getting too close!

Draw your ideas and then title them.

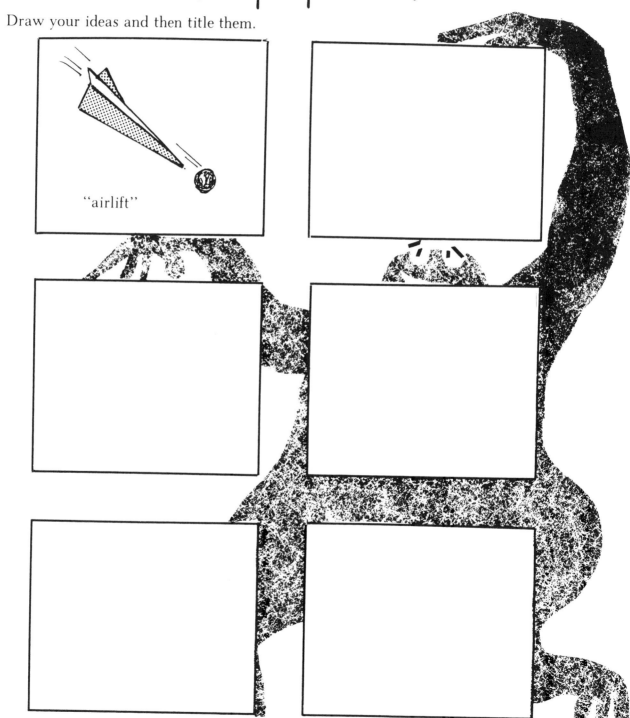

"airlift"

LIST things
that can really stick!

_____bubble gum in your eyebrows_____

_____

_____

_____

_____

_____

_____a nickname_____

_____

_____

_____

_____

_____

_____

_____

_____

_____

_____

_____

_____

_____

_____getting stuck by a swordfish_____

_____

_____

_____

_____

"A stick in the mud can really stick!"

LIST things
that would cause a hippopotamus to hyperventilate.

not being in animal cracker boxes
_____
_____
_____
_____
listening to hippopotami jokes
_____
_____
_____
_____
_____
_____
_____
determining a dinner menu for a hippogriff
_____
_____

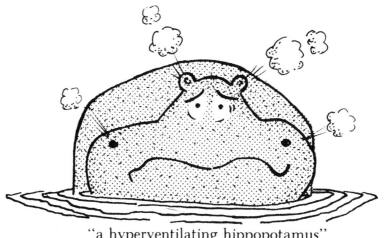

"a hyperventilating hippopotamus"

LIST things
that can get squishy!

a stomach full of soda pop and bananas

_____

_____

_____

being in love

_____

_____

_____

_____

a slow moving housefly that got swatted

_____

_____

_____

_____

_____

Which of your squishies is the squishiest? Why?

"a squishy squash"

LIST things
that go pit-a-pat!

heartbeats when I'm scared

baby partridges on a tin roof

raindrops on my head

a hippogriff coming home late at night

"A rat can go pit-a-pat

...and so can a kitty-cat!"

LIST things
that could become nubbles!

pencils

carpenters' thumbs

toothbrushes for sharks

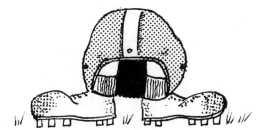

"Recovering fumbles can create a nubble!!!"

LIST things
that you feel good about!

_____
_____
_____
_____
_____
_____
_____
_____
_____
_____
_____
_____
_____
_____
_____
_____

"The most priceless collectible is a good feeling."
"Collect a few today!"

LIST things
that might become squiggles!

_____ a pocketful of worms _____

_____

_____

_____

_____

_____

_____ waiting for a report card _____

_____

_____

_____

_____

_____

_____

_____

_____

_____

Which of the above is your best "squiggle giggle"?

"A family of squiggles squiggling along!"

LIST things

_____

_____
_____
_____
_____
_____
_____
_____
_____
_____
_____
_____
_____
_____
_____
_____
_____
_____
_____
_____
_____
_____
_____

"list" idea by: _____

ATTRIBUTE LISTING

Use ATTRIBUTE LISTING for

- FACILITATING THE FLOW OF IDEAS;

- SPRINGBOARDING ORIGINALITY;

- ORGANIZING INFORMATION;

- RECLASSIFYING THINGS;

- PROMOTING A GREATER AWARENESS OF SOMETHING.

size

functions

shape

material

odor

color

taste

texture

ingredients

sound

weight

ATTRIBUTE LISTING

GETTING ORIENTED: ATTRIBUTE LISTING is the listing of qualities or characteristics of things. In doing so we look at the component parts or attributes of what a thing possesses. This process allows us to gain a greater understanding and meaning of the item under investigation for improvement purposes or for making transfer of its attributes to the improvement of somethings else.

ATTRIBUTE LISTING was developed more than 40 years ago by Robert P. Crawford at the University of Nebraska for teaching his journalism students how to think creatively. It is a great tool for developing originality in writing and coining figures of speech.

For additional information on ATTRIBUTE LISTING consult Walter G. Mettal's chapter in Angelo M. Biondi's book, **Have an Affair With Your Mind,"** (Biondi, 1974). Also consider the prime source, **Direct Creativity**, (Crawford, 1964).

GETTING STARTED: Engage your class in a general discussion on what we can use to describe things, that is, shape, size, color, weight, texture, ingredients, functions, taste, odor, etc. Indicate that it is these characteristics or attributes that add meaning to our understanding of things.

Before beginning the exercises try having students list the attributes of something they have like a pencil or a ruler. Afterwards, impress on them the great quantity of information they generated. Tell students that ATTRIBUTE LISTING activities require a considerable amount of data on whatever is being attributed.

THE ACTIVITIES:

My Best Attributes . . . This is a good activity to begin with since it personifies self with the expectations of the technique. Inform students that attributes can also describe some not so desirable characteristics of things, but in this activity they are only looking for the best attributes. Once the first page has been completed, distribute the second page which will cause somewhat of a surprise. Encourage students to use all of the attributes they listed on the first page to program the robot for a specific job.

distribute the second page which will cause somewhat of a surprise. Encourage students to use all of the attributes they listed on the first page to program the robot for a specific job.

What Are The Attributes of Superhero? . . . Figures of speech make for great creative effort. Encourage students to write descriptive words first. Words like quick, smart, honest, etc., that might describe a super person would work best. This activity should be done by the individual student and not as a total or small group exercise.

Here Are Some Attributes . . . . This activity can work well as a small group activity or as an individual student activity. Have students think of things or objects that spin and things that collect. By putting things or objects from the two separate categories together, some interesting invention ideas will emerge. The essence of this activity indicates some of the value of ATTRIBUTE LISTING for inventiveness of thought. Praise efforts!

What Are The Attributes Of A School Lunch Box? . . . . This is another individual or small group activity which demonstrates the versatililty of ATTRIBUTE LISTING. By replacing some attributes of something, interesting and surprising changes may occur. Things are improved in this fashion - from recipes to products of all types.

What Are the Attributes Of A Mushroom? . . . . Try this as an individual student exercise. That last direction on the student activity page will cause some insight as to how things in nature might suggest future possibilities. In other words, the transfer of attributes to something entirely different may create different functions for something else.

WHAT ELSE   After experiencing ATTRIBUTE LISTING activities, try the same technique with a problem. List the component parts of the problem separately; then do ATTRIBUTE LISTING on each of those parts. Brainstorm possible solutions to each attribute listed.

REFEREENCES

Crawford, Robert P. **Direct Creativity**. Wells, Vermont: Fraser, 1964.

Biondi, Angelo M. (ed.) **Have an Affair With Your Mind**, Chapter 5, "Creative Solutions through Attribute Listing," by Walter G. Mettal. Great Neck, New York: Creative Synergetic Associates, Ltd., 1974.

My Best Attributes

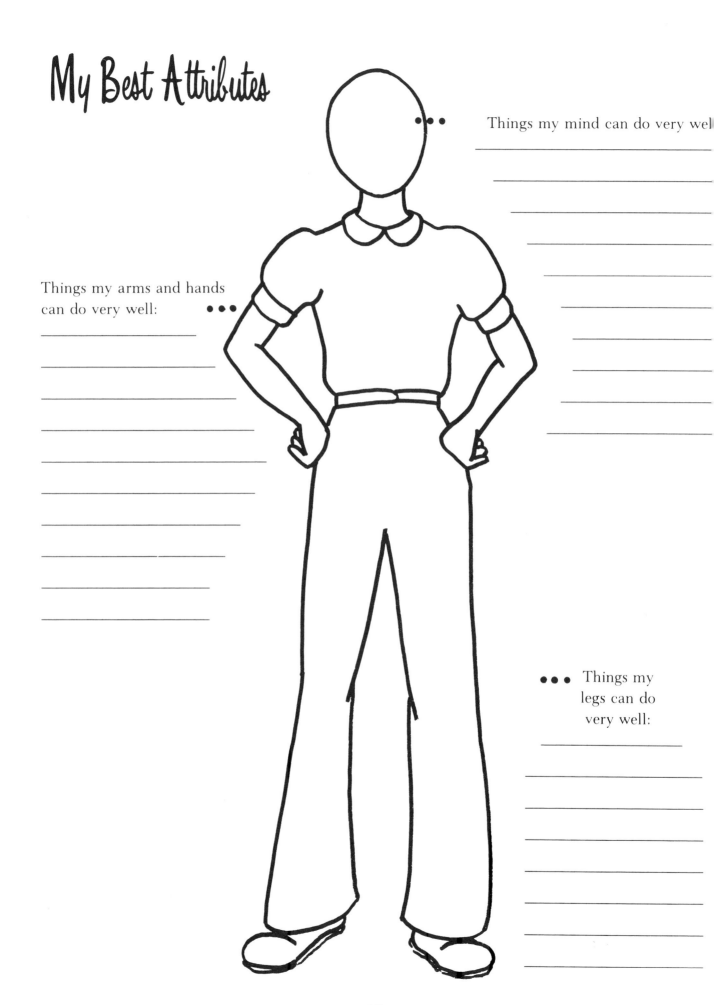

Things my mind can do very well

_____

_____

_____

_____

_____

_____

_____

Things my arms and hands
can do very well:

_____

_____

_____

_____

_____

_____

_____

Things my
legs can do
very well:

_____

_____

_____

_____

_____

_____

42

My Best Attributes

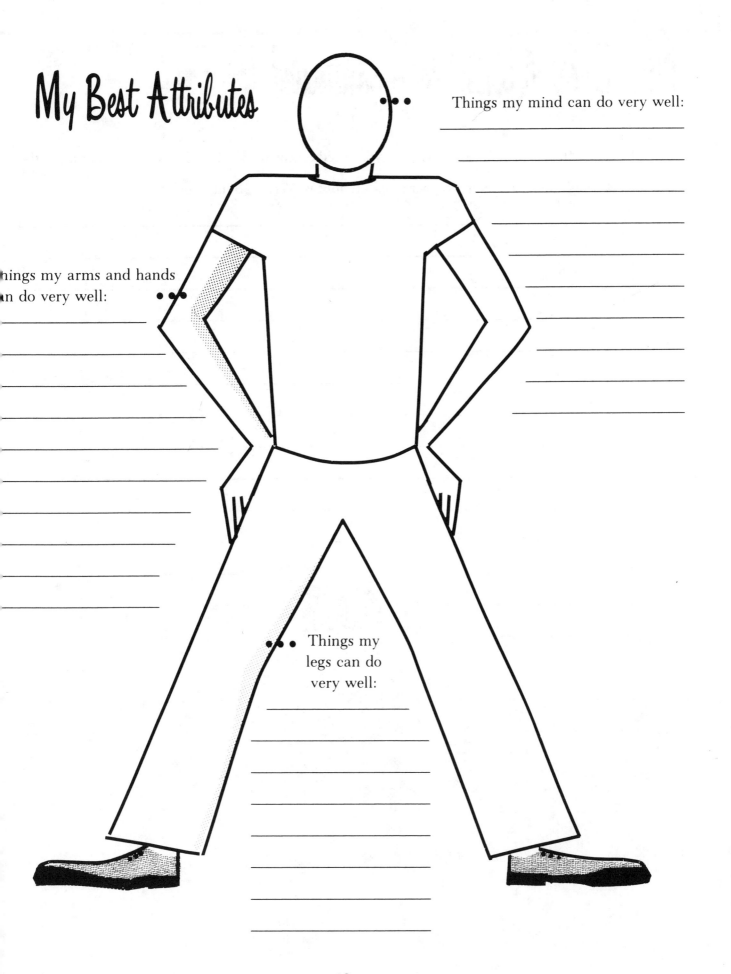

Things my mind can do very well:

_____

_____

_____

_____

Things my arms and hands can do very well:

_____

_____

_____

_____

_____

_____

Things my legs can do very well:

_____

_____

_____

_____

_____

_____

My Best Attributes – continued

Program the robot with the attributes you listed on the previous page. Now think of a job the robot could do with your programmed attributes. Write about it below:

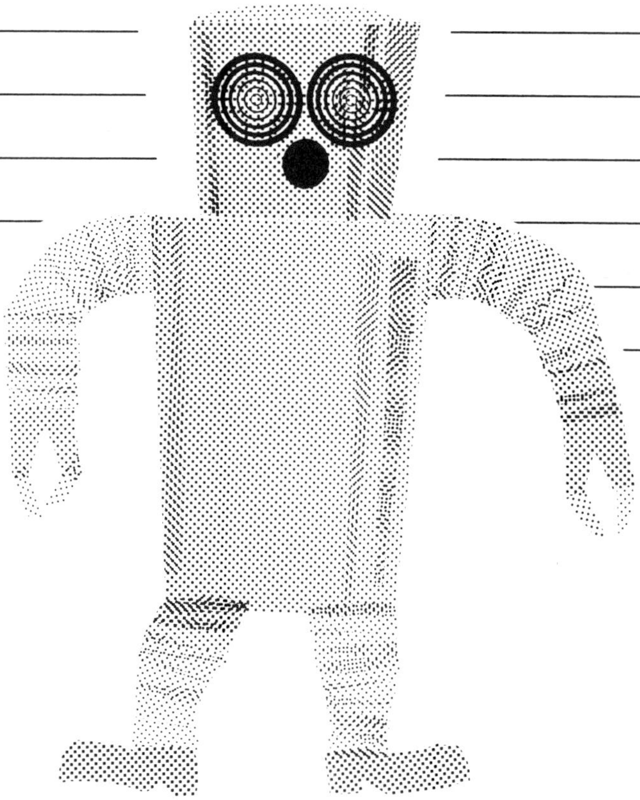

_____

_____

_____

_____

_____

_____

_____

_____

_____

_____

_____

_____

_____

_____

_____

_____

_____

What are the ATTRIBUTES of Superhero?

List the attributes as figures of speech.

STRONG AS _____ an oncoming hurricane. _____

FAST AS _____

_____

_____

_____

_____

TRUSTWORTHY AS _____

_____

_____

_____

_____

Now list a couple of attributes that would describe you. Write them as figures of speech.

_____

_____

_____

_____

_____

Here are some ATTRIBUTES!

spinning

a toy top

collecting

a magnet

1. Think of things or objects that the attributes of SPINNING and COLLECTING might describe. Write each thing or object in the appropriate attribute group.

2. Match some things or objects from the two different groups and come up with an unusual invention. Tell how each invention functions.

A toy top magnet for picking up fallen nails from the floor of a carpenter's shop

_____

_____

_____

_____

_____

_____

What are the ATTRIBUTES of a school lunch box?

shape? weight? outside appearance? material? purpose? inside appearance? size? color?

_____ a handle to carry it _____

_____

_____

_____

_____

_____

_____

_____

_____

_____

_____

Take some of the attributes you listed and replace them with something else or change them in some way.

List the changes here: _____

_____

_____

_____

In what ways were the changes an improvement?

What are the ATTRIBUTES of a mushroom?

_____ Many are shaped like umbrellas. _____

_____ There are patterns of ridges underneath. _____

_____ The material they're made of is spongy. _____

_____

_____

_____

_____

_____

_____

_____

_____

_____

_____

_____

_____

How might some of the mushroom attributes be used in designing future environments?

Use additional paper for your writing and your drawings.

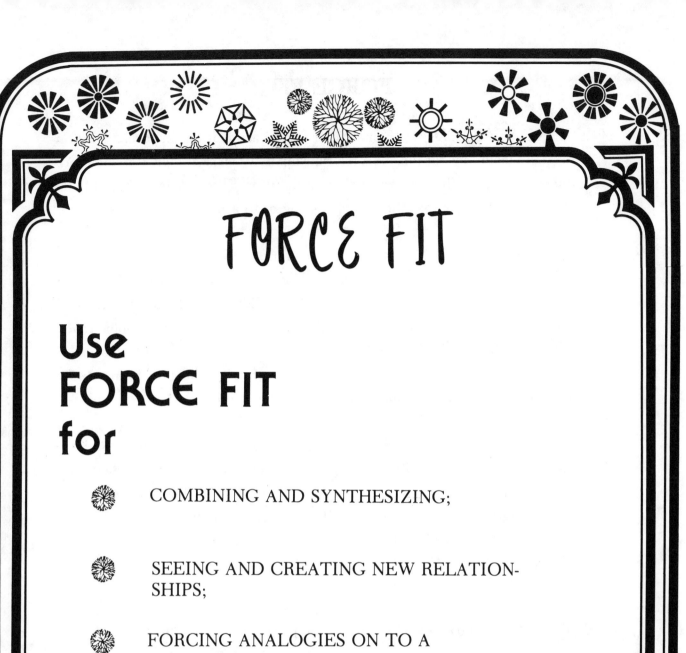

FORCE FIT

Use FORCE FIT for

- COMBINING AND SYNTHESIZING;

- SEEING AND CREATING NEW RELATION-SHIPS;

- FORCING ANALOGIES ON TO A PROBLEM.

FORCE FIT

GETTING STARTED: FORCE FIT or forced associations or forced relationships is a technique for forcing a relationship between seemingly unrelated products or ideas for the purpose of generating ideas. These ideas may lead to the improvement or the invention of something or to a problem solution.

The FORCE FIT technique has been used extensively over the years by persons whose professional careers are highly dependent upon the generation of new ideas. For classroom application refer to Edward DeBono's book, **Think Tank**, for some exciting notions of FORCE FIT. See **The Unconventional Invention Book**, (Stanish, 1981) for other adaptions. For additional information on FORCE FIT try Charles S. Whiting's book, **Creative Thinking**, (Whiting, 1958), and **Guide to Creative Action**, (Parnes, Noller and Biondi, 1977).

With all of the FORCE FIT strategies encourage students to "feel-wheel" their thoughts. The activities will promote, with some applied imagination, a way of viewing relationships among things. By viewing analogies, new understandings and information will result. It is highly recommended that some LISTING and ATTRIBUTE LISTING activity experiences occur before attempting FORCE FIT.

GETTING STARTED: Some suggested approaches are as follows:

What Was Forced To Make It Fit? Try this activity with either a small group or as an individual student exercise. Encourage students to look closely at the invention and determine all the parts. Should a discussion arise as to wheels or doughnuts on the pot, tell students it can be whatever they want it to be. Encourage students to generate a variety of uses for the invention.

Feature A Creature With A Force Fit: Most of your students have seen a recent science fiction movie on space. However, you might ask some students to provide a description of a "Star Wars" motion picture to the entire class. This activity is a three-page effort and scissors are a requirement. Encourage students to use their imaginations to construct creatures that no one else in the class would create. Display their creations and have students explain their functions in the proposed movie.

Force Fit Some Pairs of Words: This is another individual student exercise which should result in some highly original drawings and titles. Encourage students to think of rhyming words first, that is, the titles before beginning the drawings. Share individual efforts with the entire class.

One From Two: Encourage students to list several battery operated items and kitchen-type items on scratch paper before beginning this activity. After completion, have a class discussion on familiar store items that are examples of FORCE FIT.

Force Fit A Cast Of Characters: Upon completion, have students write a short story involving their created characters.

WHAT ELSE   Select at random several nouns, about ten, from a dictionary and write a definition for each word. Ask students to FORCE FIT the word function or the definition of some of the nouns to the improvement of something. Try it with a grocery cart. Suppose the noun chair was used as one of the words. The function of a chair is that of providing a place to sit. FORCE FIT the function of a chair to a shopping cart. Use several nouns and their functions for improving the item. Try the same concept with something a little more personal, like a problem. The concept of random words and their application to solving problems or improving things is the essence of FORCE FIT.

REFERENCES

DeBono, Edward E. **Think Tank**. Toronto: Think Tank Corp., 1973.

Parnes, Sidney J., Noller, Ruth B., and Biondi, Angelo M., **Guide To Creative Action**. New York: Scribner's, 1976.

Stanish, Bob. **The Unconventional Invention Book**. Carthage, Illinois: Good Apple, Inc., 1981.

Whiting, Charles S. **Creative Thinking**. New York: Reinhold Publishing Co., 1958.

Hippogriffs never get lost. They credit their accomplishment to their flight plan which is: "Any destination is attainable if you know where you've been."

What was FORCED to make it FIT?

Look at the illustration and determine what things were used in making the strange invention.

Based on what was used, determine what the invention might be used for.

things used?

invention uses?

Feature a Creature With a FORCE FIT

Imagine you had the job of creating a new character for another "Star Wars" movie.

Assemble some odd pieces for featuring a new creature from outer space in the movie.

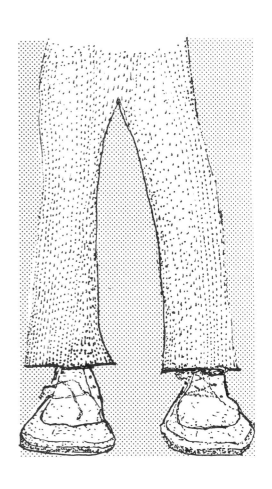

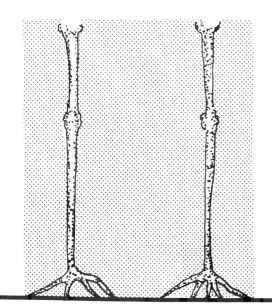

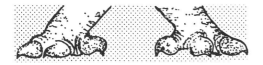

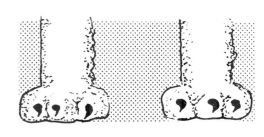

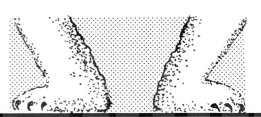

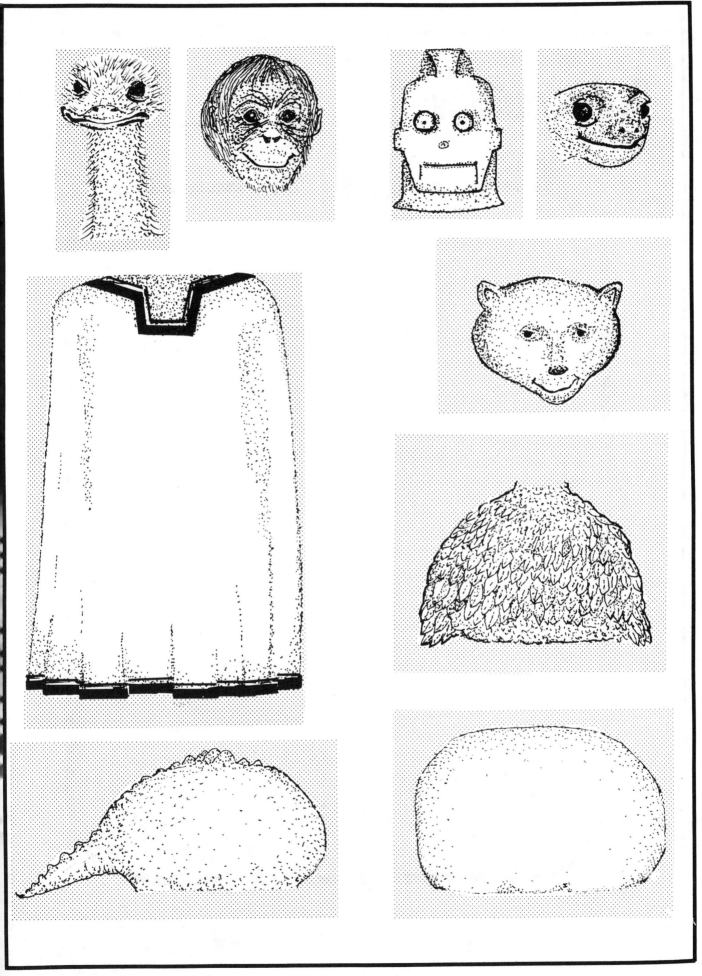

Creature created by: _____

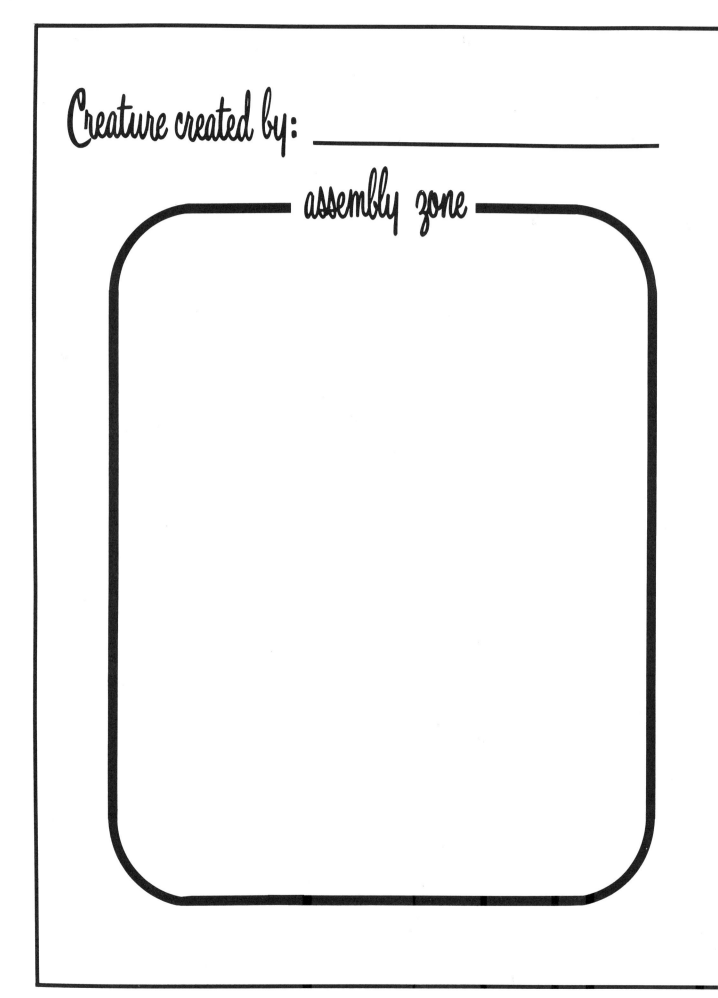

assembly zone

FORCE FIT
some pairs of words.

"A SMUG MUG"

Think of some rhyming words for an illustrated force fit!

Give a title or caption to each of your drawings.

Also write an explanation below each of the drawings.

A smug mug closes its eyes when full and opens them when empty.

One From Two

1. Write a battery operated item here: _____

2. Write a kitchen item here: _____

3. Force fit the two items to make one item and add som
wheels. Do it with a drawing!

FORCE FIT
a Cast of Characters

Cut along the dotted lines and reassemble a new cast of story characters. Paste or tape your new characters within the boxes on the second page of this activity. Give each character a name and provide a brief biographical sketch below each picture box. Use this information to write a short story.

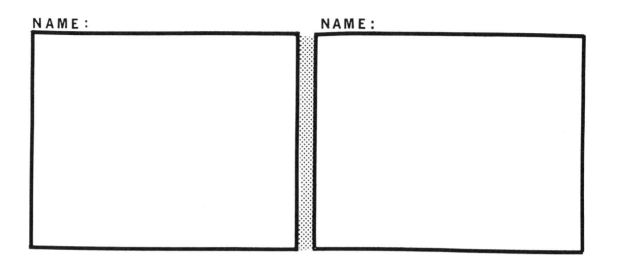

NAME:

NAME:

NAME:

NAME:

SYNECTICS – Making Metaphors

Use SYNECTICS for

    OBTAINING DIFFERENT VIEWPOINTS;

    MAKING COMPARISONS;

    SOLVING PROBLEMS;

    MAKING ANALOGIES;

    GENERATING ALTERNATIVES THROUGH SYNTHESIZING AND COMBINING.

SYNECTICS - MAKING METAPHORS

GETTING ORIENTED: SYNECTICS is a derivative of the Greek word **synecticos** and refers to the joining of unrelated elements. The significance of this concept to creative thinking is the association of facts and ideas into new configurations of interpretation and understanding.

SYNECTICS is a structured approach to problem solving. It is not the purpose of this chapter to provide the entire process, but some of the operational mechanisms have immediate application to promoting creative thinking and writing in the classroom.

Two basic processes (Prince, 1976) of SYNECTICS are:

Making the Strange Familiar -	combining something familiar with a new or unfamiliar problem to obtain a new perspective on it.
Making the Familiar Strange -	combining something strange to something familiar in order to gain a new perspective on it.

There are three operational mechanisms (Synectics, Inc., 1968) which deliberately Make the Familiar Strange:

1. Direct Analogy (simple comparison)
2. Personal Analogy (being the thing)
3. Symbolic Analogy (compressed conflict)

This chapter will feature activities which promote the use of the three operational mechanisms.

Direct Analogies are simple comparisons of one thing to something else. That is, two objects are compared. There is much more value in having a greater strain between two compared objects than having a close relationship. The greater the strain between two objects the more effective it becomes in MAKING THE FAMILIAR STRANGE. Comparing a teaspoon with a smile is a far greater analytical instrument than the comparison of a teaspoon with a shovel. By using or by causing a strain or a distant relationship between two objects for viewing comparisons, we broaden our perspectives to accommodate varying points of view.

The purpose of the Direct Analogy is to gain access to the metaphor - a great instrument for enhancing our knowledge about the world.

Personal Analogies simply involve a personal identification with a thing. This personification includes the feelings, the parts, and the function of the item. In many instances it is like the placement of ourselves into the essence of a problem or into the things being investigated.

There is a big difference between the concept of role playing and Personal-Analogy strategies. To put oneself in the place of another person and dramatize how that individual might respond to a particular situation or event is role playing. Personal-Analogy activities might include becoming an electron or a jammed door lock. Imagining how we might react if we were the thing provides insight into the subject. It also provides us with a means of adding facts and information to that phase of problem solving which is essential to any solution, that is, fact-finding.

A Symbolic Analogy is a two-word statement containing conflict. The conflict is created by using antonyms. The words must, literally, fight each other to produce the conflict. For example, a phrase like "deafening silence " is a Symbolic Analogy.

Symbolic Analogies have certain characteristics: the words have a poetic stretch; the words have a broad meaning which can be applied to many different situations and the internal conflict inherent in the statement. Of the three types of analogies, Symbolic Analogy provides the broadest insight into the content of things. Its development is essentially analytical. The paradoxes which provide the content of Symbolic Analogies are found everywhere. They are common to the world.

Symbolic Analogies are difficult for younger children. It is suggested that this type of strategy be reserved for students in the fourth grade and above.

The pioneering work of W. J. J. Gordon (Gordon, 1961) and George M. Prince and the Synectics Corporation have established Synectics as a prime operational process in problem solving. As indicated earlier, what is included in this chapter does not detail the entire Synectics program. But what is included are some of the mechanisms from the process that can help anyone, especially children, in becoming much more adept at thinking and writing creatively.

GETTING STARTED: Begin with selecting one of these Direct-Analogy strategies:

How Is Laughter Like A Smudge Of Peanut Butter? This activity indicates the Direct-Analogy type of comparison, that is, promoting a strain or a distant relationship between two objects. Create teams of two, three, or four students for expanding metaphorical thinking with this activity. Share results after completion.

How Loud Is Loud? The concept of loud is expanded here to entertain different viewpoints. Assure students that there are no "wrong" answers here. It all depends on a viewing platform that can be altered easily. Try this as an individual activity and look for analytical thinking. There should be plenty of it!

How Squashy Is It? This is another individual type of activity which gets into even further expansion of differing viewpoints. You should receive some very interesting perspectives. See if student reactions match your own perceptions of those students.

Here are the Personal-Analogy strategies:

Be A Hot Air Balloon: Duplicate all four pages of this activity and distribute to students. This activity is structured visually to motivate what it would be like to be a hot air balloon. Try it as an individual student activity if a quiet time of twenty minutes can prevail. Afterwards, look for feeling responses and personification with the object. Also, ask students to describe the type of day, wind currents, and other weather elements they encountered on their trip.

As an alternative to duplication, try making overhead projector transparencies and projecting the activity illustrations as large as possible on a wall. Encourage silence until student-written reactions are fully completed.

Ask, "What things on earth might be viewed more effectively from an elevation of a few thousand feet than from ground level? If we had an automatic viewer lens for looking down on things, what would be worth looking at? In what ways would this help in our understanding of things?"

Personal Analogies make for great approaches to creative writing. Here's another one similar to the last one:

Be A Piece Of Driftwood On A White Water Stream: Before distributing this activity, have a general discussion on white water streams and rivers. Point out that white water makes for great canoeing and raft trips. White water can be treacherous because of the rocks and requires skill to navigate downstream. Also, discuss the beauty of driftwood and how many people landscape their lawns with it or use it indoors for centerpieces on tables or with flower arrangements or for candlestick holders.

On the third page of this activity, students are asked to conclude both in writing and in drawing how their story ends. This should make for some interesting viewing and storytelling. Be sure to allow time for both in a session of group sharing.

Ask students to provide as many different viewpoints as possible to driftwood from varying sources: "How would a stream view driftwood? How would an artist view driftwood? How would a camper view driftwood? How would a manager of a beach resort view driftwood? How would the earth view driftwood?"

The next Personal-Analogy activity is not a creative writing one, but it can show emphatically the tremendous creative potential of the process:

Be A Chameleon And Change Colors: Although an individual student approach would be fine, consider teams of two for more creative production. One of the significant values of Synectics is to search out how nature did it in searching for problem solutions. This activity demonstrates vividly how it can work!

Be A Raindrop And Fall Into A Puddle Of Water: This activity can, as an alternative, be dramatized with student movement in a nonverbal rendition. If you do it this way, just read the script with a few alterations in the wording. Conclude with a verbal discussion on the last statement.

Either way, creative movement or creative writing, the essence of the activity is "a raindrop is like _____ because . . . . ."

Begin the Symbolic-Analogy strategies with:

Best Sellers: Whatever book titles students come up with will have some poetic stretch. Using paired antonyms will create conflict and will cause a poetic stretch. Try this exercise as an individual student activity and encourage students to "play around" with the right combination of words for the best opposing meaning. This can be accomplished by thinking of synonyms associated with each word. Students should have fun with this activity. Use the activity as a lead-in to the others that follow, since it introduces the concept of compressed conflict.

Revoltingly Appealing Is Super Sundae: Tell students that the activity title is much like the book titles they created on "Best Sellers." Conflict is compressed by using paired words of opposite meanings. Use the activity as an individual student effort and urge students when putting together the recipe not to include things that are indigestible to human taste. Urge them to think, rather, in terms of color, size, and calorie intake as potential revolting factors in the sundae creation.

The key element in this activity is the last statement which requires a transfer of concept to real-life situations. Encourage students to think about their own life experiences which could be described as "revoltingly appealing."

Inattentive Concentration: Use the metaphor associated with the drawing as a lead-in for the activity. This exercise will require some student deliberation and provide time for it. You might suggest the traditional "poker-game" unexpressive facial expression as an example of inattentive concentration and how "dumb-smart" might be used to gain an advantage in a certain situation.

REFERENCES

Gordon, W.J.J. **Synectics**. New York: Harper & Row, 1961.

Synectics, Inc., **Making It Strange**. New York: Harper & Row, 1968.

How is Laughter Like a Smudge of Peanut Butter?

Sometimes it's hard to swallow.

Can't use either one in study hall.

How Loud is Loud?

Which is louder?

      having the attention of a crowd of people

      being ignored

Why? _____

_____

_____

_____

_____

_____

_____

_____

Think of something else that is loud.

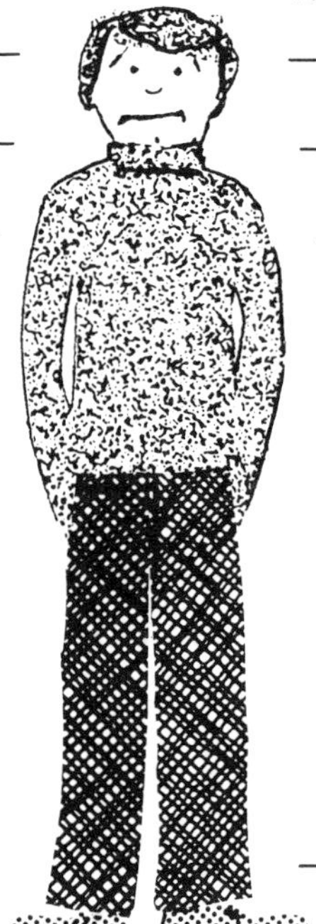

_____

_____

_____

_____

_____

_____

_____

_____

Think of something else that is even louder!

_____

_____

_____

_____

_____

_____

_____

How Squashy is it?

Which is squashier?

      a sack of broken eggs

      getting praised in public

Why? _____

_____

_____

_____

_____

Which is squashier?

      an overdrawn bank account

      getting sat upon by a small elephant

Why? _____

_____

_____

_____

_____

Add things to this illustration that might cause a
small elephant to get
up from a couch!

Be a Hot Air Balloon

Draw a design on yourself.

Take an early morning flight!

Be a Hot Air Balloon — continued

Use your blast valve and feel the hot air inside of you. Write about your thoughts and feelings as you go up!

Be a Hot Air Balloon — continued

3. Feel the gentle winds guide you and the warmth of the morning sun.

4. Write about your thoughts and feelings.

Be a Hot Air Balloon — continued

5. Describe your thoughts and feelings as you become heavier and float softly back to earth.

Be a Piece of Driftwood
on a White Water Stream

1. Describe your experiences as you travel downstream.

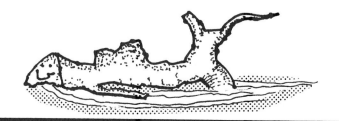

Be a Piece of Driftwood on a White Water Stream - cont.

.. You have wood-wrecked on an island of rock!
Describe your frustration as you long for the stream.

3. Describe how your story ends!

4. Do a drawing!

Be a Chameleon and Change Colors

Be a dark color or a light color or something in between! Imagine what it would be like changing colors! Take a few minutes and just think about it!

Imagine you are a chameleon. Imagine that you could transfer some of your magic powers of changing colors to some person-made products. What would you select? What would the benefits be?

WHAT?	BENEFITS?
a roof	Become black in winter to absorb heat and white in summer to reflect heat.

Be a Raindrop
and Fall into a Puddle of Water

Write about your thoughts and feelings

as a falling raindrop

as a particle of water in a water puddle

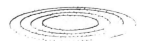

Be a Raindrop – continued

The sun comes out and you soon evaporate. Now you are air. You travel in air currents across continents and sometimes in strong winds that cause damage. Tell about one of your journeys as a particle of air.

Under a cloud you condense and become a raindrop again. Now think about this: A raindrop is like _____ because:

Best Sellers

A good book contains conflict which will hold the reader's interest.

A good book title which reflects conflict can mean good sales. Try creating some make-believe book titles by compressing conflict. Conflict can be compressed by using words of opposite meanings in combination. See the example at the bottom of the book stack.

Write your titles and authors right on the book covers illustrated below.

COLD FIRE by I.M. KULBLAZE

Revoltingly Appealing is Super Sundae

Give some directions for making a super sundae that is both revolting and appealing.

What would make it revolting?

What would make it appealing?

Describe a real-life situation which could be titled "Revoltingly Appealing!"

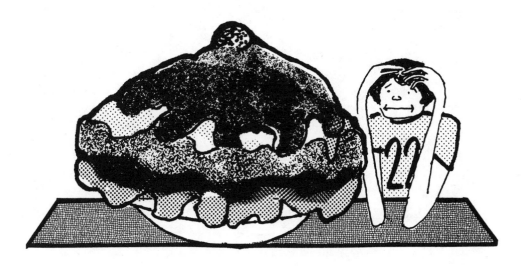

Inattentive Concentration

Imagine you won something through "inattentive concentration." Make up a story.

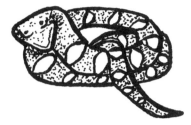

Inattentive concentration is like a copperhead snake lying lazily in the summer sun, that is, until something crosses its path!

UP FRONT & PERSONAL

or

HIPPOGRIFF ENCOUNTERS

ORIGINALITY is

BREAKING AWAY FROM HABIT-BOUND THINKING AND

- PRODUCING PRODUCTS OF NOVELTY;

- THINKING UNCONVENTIONALLY;

- GETTING INVOLVED ON SEVERAL LEVELS OF CONSCIOUSNESS;

- COMING UP WITH SOLUTIONS THAT OTHERS DO NOT THINK OF.

HIPPOGRIFF ENCOUNTERS

GETTING ORIENTED: Creativity tests indicate a high correlation between fluency and originality of around .60. Measures of originality, however, usually predict creative behavior more accurately than do measures of fluency (Torrance, 1972; 1974). Recall some of the LISTING activities and check if the more fluent students affirm the correlation with originality which is featured in this chapter.

A rather consistent finding in creativity research has been that responses on creativity tests are somewhat less original during the first few minutes than those during the latter minutes. This may be due to the needed warm-up to the process. Extend your classroom planning to include consistent and periodic accommodation of student originality. Provide a warm-up to those activities that deal with originality. Implement humor whenever you can. Humor will loosen self-imposed constraints that we all deal with when facing new situations.

E. Paul Torrance (Torrance, 1979) suggests a need for curricular planning to extend the accommodation of student originality. Extend the activities in this chapter as much as you can and develop ones of your own. Originality can be enhanced. Do it!

In looking for student originality in your classoom, look for:

- a desire to seek out alternative solutions to a problem;

- a heightening concern over a subject or a problem. Originality requires an emotional and mental commitment to something. Look for persistence in problem solving;

- ideas and solutions to problems that others do not think of;

- written stories that have unusual or surprising plots;

- the production of an answer or a problem solution when no one else can;

- inventiveness in constructing class products. The use of materials to produce novel, unusual, one of a kind items;

- made-up or created words to facilitate expression;

and

- a desire to challenge accepted ways of doing things; seeks out ways to improve things.

GETTING STARTED: The following activities accommodate and nurture originality in thinking:

Write Some Hippogriffitti: Look for unusual or novel graffiti (originality). Look for quantity of responses (fluency). Look for descriptive and detailed graffiti (elaboration). Look for different categories of thought (flexibility). The two examples on the activity page would fit flexibility since "hugging" a hippogriff and taking one out to "lunch" are different categories of thinking.

There Is Room For One More: The indicator here on originality is within the legend. Look for an emotional and intellectual commitment to something. See if it reflects your impressions of who are the most original thinkers. Also use this activity to gain more information about the personalities and the self-esteem levels of your class.

Attract A Hiffogriff With A Deluxe Hippogriff Tree House: Look for unique and novel designs on this one. Keep in mind that the IDEAS are the important thing here, NOT ARTISTIC TALENT. Look for other indicators of the creative processes, such as elaboration and flexibility (other categories of thought, for example, things included other than just the house).

Improve A Hippogriff Feeder: As a warm-up, go over the CHECKLIST questions on page 10. Have students offer suggestions through a general class discussion on how a hippogriff feeder could be improved by PUTTING IT TO OTHER USES - MAKING ADAPTIONS - MAKING MODIFICATIONS - BY MAGNIFYING IT - BY MINIFYING IT - BY SUBSTITUTING SOMETHING ELSE - BY REARRANGING PARTS- BY REVERSING PARTS - BY COMBINING IT WITH SOMETHING ELSE. The improvements should be interesting to share. Look for the highly original students to discard the illustration and start from scratch. If that happens, great!

Design A Hippogriff T-Shirt: Encourage students to draw their t-shirt design right on the illustrated shirt. Don't provide too much help or levy expectations. Give them a full rein and share final results with total group. Discuss originality in t-shirt designs and what makes them popular.

Design A Hippogriff On A Cliff: There are reasons why hippogriffs have not been pictured in this book. The intent is to cause visualization to happen. Now, with this activity, students will have the opportunity to demonstrate how their imaginations have expanded and developed. Encourage students to add (elaboration) things to their hippogriffs to make them special!

This activity also contains a special exercise in perception. Check out students who drew the hippogriff on the shaded area and those who drew it on the white. See if you can draw some conclusions.!

Help A Hippogriff: This exercise in problem solving can be handled in a couple of ways. Try using it with teams of two's or as an individual student activity. Expect some highly clever ways of solving this problem, like placing life jackets on the hippogriff and filling the hole with water until it is reachable or by placing gravel in the hole as a staircase method for getting the hippogriff out of the hole. This is a good activity for receiving some highly original thoughts.

Use this activity before presenting "There's a Hiffogriff on Middle Peak Mountain Who's Afraid to Come Down!" That activity requires the creation of a criteria. "Help a Hippogriff" makes a nice lead-in to it.

Was That A Flying Hippogriff? Look for some out-of-the-ordinary expressions. Provide some sharing time since even the nonartists in the class will achieve some pretty good drawings.

Sometime try this activity on student book reports or book reviews. Just cut out or eliminate the written information on the activity page and have students provide three different reviews with expressions to match from three different frames of references. Use famous personalities from their social studies or science books or from current events. Select names that would have conflicting points of view and depict how they might react to the story or book.

Chain Reaction: Look for original ideas on this problem-solving activity. Don't allow the hippogriff to fly down for it - that's out-of-bounds!

There's A Hippogriff On Middle Peak Mountain Who's Afraid To Come Down: Let students do this activity on their own. Just provide copies of the IDEA RATING GUIDE on page 9. This will be a good assessment of their abilities to establish criteria to rate ideas. Do it as an individual student activity.

Be The Only Hippogriff In Captivity - Write A Story: Make this the last Hippogriff encounter. Check out this personal analogy for student emotional reactions.

As a follow-up, deal with the importance of human empathy towards others, for example, dwarfism, mental and physical handicaps and other things that set apart dramatically some individuals from the mainstream. Talk about the commonality of human feeling and how feelings can hurt more than the other liabilities we carry.

WHAT ELSE Continue the hippogriff theme with activities from your own magic. With media presenting the total image of things to us day in and day out, you will find it refreshing, and so will your students. Construct your hippogriff encounters with care and love, for they are very special!

REFERENCES

Torrance, E. Paul, **Journal of Creative Behavior**. "Predictive Validity of the Torrance Tests of Creative Thinking," 1972, pp. 236-252.

Torrance, E. Paul, **The Torrance Tests of Creative Thinking**. (Manual, Test B) Lexington, Massachusetts: Ginn 1974.

Torrance, E. Paul, **The Search for Satori and Creativity**. Great Neck, New York: Creative Synergetic Associates, Ltd., 1979.

Hippogriffs believe that unreality is the threshold of reality!

Write Some Hippogriffitti!

HUG A
HIPPOGRIFF!
453-2667

TAKE A HUNGRY
HIPPOGRIFF TO
LUNCH!
453-2667

There is Room for One More!

There are a few who believe that a talented, strong beaked hippogriff was the real sculptor of the Mt. Rushmore faces. Draw your face next to Teddy and Abe as an artistic hippogriff would sculpture it.

In the space below, create a legend about yourself. Include things that you would like to acccomplish.

Attract a
Hippogriff With a

Deluxe
Hippogriff Tree house

Improve a Hippogriff Feeder

Make the present one better or design a new one!

decorative disposable feed trough

front talon perch

rear hoof platform

$59.99

Design a Hippogriff T-Shirt

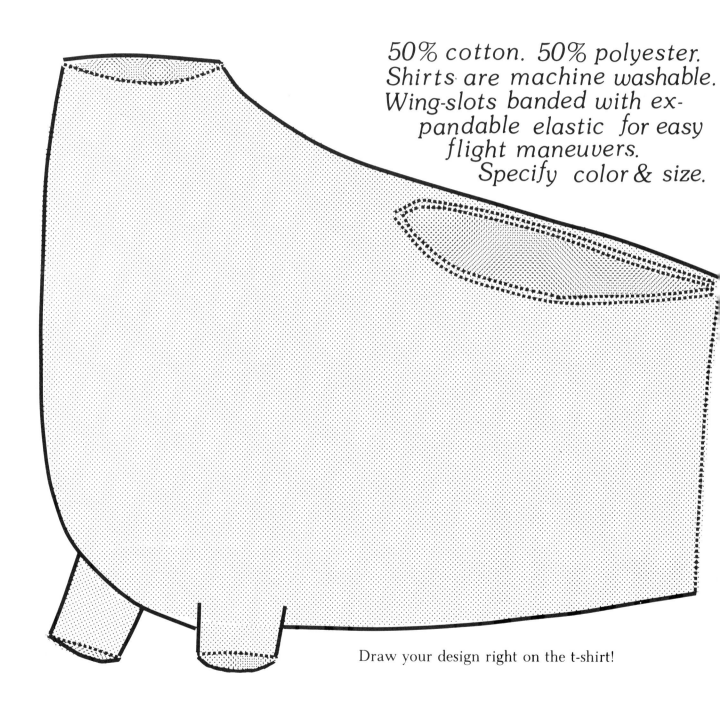

50% cotton. 50% polyester.
Shirts are machine washable.
Wing-slots banded with ex-
pandable elastic for easy
flight maneuvers.
Specify color & size.

Draw your design right on the t-shirt!

Draw a Hippogriff on a Cliff

Add some special effects!

grif·fin *(grif´ən) n. Greek Mythology.* A fabulous beast with the head and wings of an eagle and the body of a lion.

hip·po·griff *(hip´ə-grif´) n.* also **hip·po·gryph.** A mythological monster having the wings, claws, and head of a griffin and the body and hindquarters of a horse.

Help a Hippogriff!

You are in charge of a rescue mission to get an injured 300 pound hippogriff out of a deep hole.

Your immediate assessment of the situation is that the hole is 10 feet deep and 10 feet wide; the hippogriff's injury appears to be in the wings; its size is approximately 3½ feet high and 5 feet in length. The hippogriff is frightened and appears to need medical attention.

List your ideas and rate them for the best solution. Write some wild ideas, too!

IDEAS	CHANCE OF SUCCESS?	AVAILABLE EQUIPMENT?	TIME?	LOW COST?	SAFETY?	SCORING COLUMN

CRITERIA

Was that a Flying Hippogriff?

Put some facial expressions on these onlookers!

Now match their facial expressions with some thoughts!

Chain Reaction

The squirrel drops a nut on the beaver's tail who flips it to the pelican. The pelican flies the nut to the hippogriff cave. Everything is fine except the squirrel, at times, is absentminded and forgets to start the chain reaction.

Add, modify, or eliminate things in the picture to make the chain reaction more consistent.

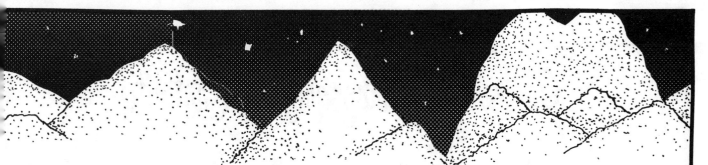

Use "The Idea Rating Guide" for a rescue solution.

Write your best solution here:

There's a Hippogriff on Middle Peak Mt.
Who's Afraid to Come Down!

Be the Only Hippogriff in Captivity

Write a story...

BIBLIOGRAPHY

Barron, Frank. **Creativity and Personal Freedom.** New York: Van Nostrand Reinhold, 1968.

Bingham, Alma. **Improving Children's Facility in Problem Solving.** New York: Bureau of Publications, Teachers College, Columbia University, 1963.

Biondi, Angelo M., ed. **Have an Affair with Your Mind.** Great Neck, New York: Creative Synergetic Associates, Ltd., 1974.

Biondi, Angelo M., ed. **The Creative Process.** Buffalo, New York: D.O.K. Publishers, 1973.

Crawford, Robert R. **Direct Creativity.** Wells, Vermont: Fraser, 1964.

Davis, Gary A. **Psychology of Problem Solving.** New York: Basic Books, 1972.

DeBono, Edward E. **Think Tank.** Toronto: Think Tank Corp., 1973.

DeBono, Edward E. **Lateral Thinking, Creativity Step by Step.** New York: Harper and Row, 1973.

Eberle, Bob. **Scamper: Games for Imagination Development.** Buffalo, New York: D.O.K. Publishers, 1971.

Eberle, Bob, and Stanish, Bob. **CPS for Kids: A Resource Book for Teaching Creative Problem-Solving to Children.** Buffalo, New York: D.O.K. Publishers, 1980.

Edwards, Betty. **Drawing on the Right Side of the Brain.** Los Angeles, California: J.P. Tarcher, Inc., 1979.

Gordon, W.J.J. **Synectics.** New York: Harper and Row, 1961.

Gowan, John Curtis. **Development of the Creative Individual.** San Diego, California: Knapp Publishers, 1972.

Gowan, John Curtis. **Trance, Art, and Creativity.** Buffalo, New York: The Creative Education Foundation, 1975.

Guilford, J.P. **Way Beyond the IQ.** Buffalo, New York: The Creative Education Foundation, 1977.

Guilford, J.P. **The Nature of Human Intelligence.** New York: McGraw-Hill, 1967.

Holland, Margaret, and Strickland, Alison. **The Listing Book.** Columbus, Ohio: School Book Fairs, 1978.

Holland, Margaret, and Strickland, Alison. **Making Movies in Your Mind.** Columbus, Ohio: School Book Fairs, 1980

Hudgins, Bryce B. **Problem Solving in the Classroom.** New York: Macmillan, 1966.

MacKinnon, Donald W. **In Search of Human Effectiveness, Identifying and Developing Creativity.** Buffalo, New York: The Creative Education Foundation, 1978.

Noller, Ruth B. **Scratching the Surface of Creative Problem Solving, A Bird's Eye View of CPS.** Buffalo, New York: D.O.K. Publishers, 1977.

Noller, Ruth B., Treffinger, Donald J., and Houseman, Elwood D. **It's a Gas to be Gifted, or CPS for the Gifted and Talented.** Buffalo, New York: D.O.K. Publishers, 1979.

Noller, Ruth B., Parnes, Sidney J., and Biondi, Angelo M. **Creative Actionbook.** Scribner's, 1976.

Osborn, Alex F. **Applied Imagination** (3rd Ed.). New York: Scribner's, 1963.

Parnes, Sidney J. **Aha, Insights into Creative Behavior.** Buffalo, New York: D.O.K. Publishers, 1975.

Parnes, Sidney J., Noller, Ruth B., and Biondi, Angelo M. **Guide to Creative Action.** New York: Scribner's, 1976.

Renzulli, Joseph S. **New Dimensions in Creativity,** Volumes Mark 1, Mark 2, and Mark 3. New York: Harper and Row, 1973.

Stanish, Bob. **The Unconventional Invention Book: Classroom Activities for Activating Student Inventiveness.** Carthage, Illinois: Good Apple, Inc., 1981.

Stanish, Bob. **I Believe in Unicorns: Classroom Experiences for Activating Creative Thinking.** Carthage, Illinois: Good Apple, Inc., 1979.

Stanish, Bob. **Sunflowering: Thinking, Feeling, Doing Activities for Creative Expression.** Carthage, Illinois: Good Apple, Inc., 1977.

Strickland, Alison, and Holland, Margaret. **Crazy Connections.**Columbus, Ohio: School Book Fairs, 1980.

Torrance, E. Paul. **The Search for Satori and Creativity.**Buffalo, New York: The Creative Education Foundation, 1979.

Torrance, E. Paul. **Guiding Creative Talent.** Englewood Cliffs, New Jersey: Prentice-Hall, 1962.

Torrance, E. Paul. **Rewarding Creative Behavior.** Englewood Cliffs, New Jersey: Prentice-Hall, 1965.

Torrance, E. Paul and Meyers, Robert E. **Creative Learning and Teaching.** New York: Harper and Row, 1970.

Wayman, Joe, and Plum, Lorraine. **Secrets and Surprises.**Carthage, Illinois: Good Apple, Inc., 1977.

Wayman, Joe. **The Other Side of Reading.** Carthage, Illinois: Good Apple, Inc., 1980.

Williams, Frank E. **A Total Creativity Program for Individualizing and Humanizing the Learning Process.** Englewood Cliffs, New Jersey: Educational Technology Publications, 1972.

Williams, Frank E. **Classroom Ideas for Encouraging Thinking and Feeling.** Buffalo, New York: D.O.K. Publishers, 1970.

Hippogriffs do not have a spoken language. Their written language is called Hippogriffitti!

The Growing Family of Good Apple Products and Services Includes

4 Periodicals to Meet the Needs of Educators

BIG, Beautiful Activities That Work as Hard as You Do

The Good Apple Newspaper, for grades 2-8, offers practical ready-to-use reproducibles, seasonal activities, posters, games and ideas. Our working teacher /authors know how to motivate and reinforce basic skills. Let us brighten your classroom and challenge young minds. Bigger, more colorful, and free of outside advertising, *The Good Apple Newspaper* is your best value in teaching publications.

Timesaving Ideas Ready to "Challenge" the Gifted!

Challenge provides you with ready-to-use creative and critical thinking activities, articles from leaders in gifted education and features to help parents of gifted students. Inspiring interviews, thought-provoking games and complete units of study provide you with in-depth materials to "challenge" the academic, physical, mechanical and artistically gifted child.

Teachers Love Lollipops!

Lollipops magazine is especially for teachers of preschool-grade 2. Each issue includes stories and poems, calendars, bulletin boards, value-related materials, a full-color poster and more. The seasonal focus of each issue provides you with learning material children will love.

Finally! A Ready-to-Use Teaching Magazine

Oasis magazine, from Good Apple, is packed full of timesaving, skill-building activities and ideas just for you—the busy teacher of grades 5-9. Reproducibles, activities, teacher tips, full-color posters, calendars and reviews are all age and curriculum appropriate! With more you'll really use and no outside advertising, there's no better value in a classroom magazine.

Good Apple Idea and Activity Books

In all subject areas for all grade levels, preschool-grade 8+. Idea books, activity books, bulletin board books, units of instruction, reading, creativity, readiness, gameboards, science, math, social studies, responsibility education, self-concept, gifted, seasonal ideas, arts/crafts, poetry, language arts and teacher helpers.

Activity Posters • Note Pads • Software • Videos

Teachers Publishing for Teachers